Fact Finders®

ENGINEERING WONDERS

THE GREAT PYRAMID OF GIZA

BY REBECCA STANBOROUGH

CAPSTONE PRESS
a capstone imprint

Fact Finders Books are published by Capstone Press,
1710 Roe Crest Drive, North Mankato, Minnesota 56003
www.mycapstonepub.com

Library of Congress Cataloging-in-Publication Data
Names: Stanborough, Rebecca, author.
Title: The great pyramid of Giza / by Rebecca Stanborough.
Other titles: Fact finders. Engineering wonders.
Description: North Mankato, Minn.: Capstone Press, 2016. | Series: Fact
  finders. Engineering wonders | Includes bibliographical references.
Identifiers: LCCN 2015035327|
  ISBN 978-1-4914-8195-0 (library binding)
  ISBN 978-1-4914-8199-8 (paperback)
  ISBN 978-1-4914-8203-2 (ebook pdf)
Subjects: LCSH: Great Pyramid (Egypt)—Juvenile literature.
  Egypt—Civilization—To 332 B.C.—Juvenile literature.
Classification: LCC DT63 .S679 2016 | DDC 932—dc23

Editorial Credits
Elizabeth Johnson and Gena Chester, editors; Veronica Scott, designer;
Svetlana Zhurkin, media researcher; Lori Barbeau, production specialist

Photo Credits
Alamy: age fotostock, 17; Bridgeman Images: Peter Jackson Collection/Look and Learn/Private Collection/Building the Great Pyramid at Giza (gouache on paper), Jackson, Peter (1922-2003), 20; Getty Images: Dorling Kindersley, 19; Granger, NYC, cover; Newscom: akg-images/Andrea Jemolo, 6, Danita Delimont Photography/Kenneth Garrett, 22, Prisma/Album, 27, Universal Images Group/De Agostini Picture Library, 7, 25; Shutterstock: Brian Maudsley, 26, Danita Delmont, 5, Frank11, 13, Gurgen Bakhshetsyan, 10, mareandmare, 8, oriontrail, 15, pavalena, 11 (bottom), Pius Lee, 11 (top), Sphinx Wang, 28—29; Wikimedia: CaptMondo, 12, Einsamer Schutze, 9

Design Elements by Shutterstock

Printed in the United States of America, in North Mankato.
007539CGS16

TABLE OF CONTENTS

CHAPTER 1

A GREAT PYRAMID

In the Fourth Dynasty of Egypt (2575 BC to 2465 BC), the **Pharaoh** Khufu decided to build a pyramid. It would rise, dazzling and white, from the desert sand to show that Khufu was an important ruler. The Egyptians also believed the pyramid would help Khufu protect them—even after he died.

By Khufu's time, Egyptian pharaohs had already built many pyramids. Each new pharaoh learned from the previous projects. Even so, the Great Pyramid of Giza is a wonder. The base of the pyramid is **level** to within 1 inch (2.5 centimeters). The four sides of the pyramid line up almost perfectly with the north, east, south, and west directions. The sides are almost exactly the same length.

The Great Pyramid was built more than 4,000 years ago. Its beauty and history attract millions of visitors every year. The Great Pyramid is also an **engineering** wonder.

pharaoh—a king of ancient Egypt
level—to make flat
engineering—using science to design and build things

4

Did You Know?

The Great Pyramid is so perfectly designed that people sometimes say aliens must have helped!

The Egyptians used the sky, earth, and river, as well as their tools, machines, and building skills to create this marvel of engineering. People are still in awe of the Egyptians who imagined, planned, and built it.

The Great Pyramid was called "the horizon of Khufu"—the place where Khufu rises and sets.

5

Pyramids were built as tombs for pharaohs. They protected the pharaoh's **mummified** body. They also held the supplies he would need in the afterlife. The pyramid shape symbolized the rays of the sun. Pyramids are very stable buildings. They have four sides. Their triangular sides are stronger than rectangular sides. And they can be built to great heights, as long as the base is wide enough. The pyramids were meant to stand until the end of time. They have even survived earthquakes!

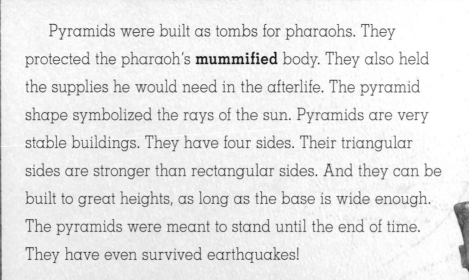

Did You Know?

The only statue of Khufu in existence is the smallest piece of Egyptian royal sculpture ever discovered. It is an ivory statue only 3 inches (7.5 cm) high.

mummify—to preserve a body with special salts and cloth to make it last for a very long time

THE SACRED JOURNEY: THE PYRAMID AS PHARAOH'S LADDER

Ancient Egyptians believed strongly in the afterlife. They thought that a person's *ka*, or life-force, lived on after his or her body died. The ka needed to be kept healthy, so Egyptians placed food, drink, and other supplies in their tombs.

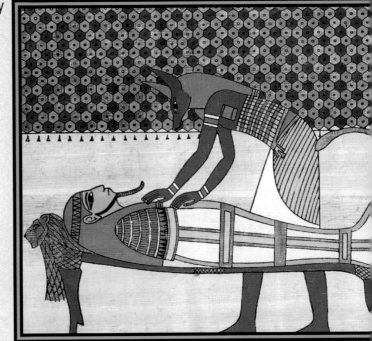

The *ba*, or soul, needed a body in which to rest. That is why the Egyptians mummified the dead. After a pharaoh died, his ba and ka could travel to the heavens and become a god. As a god, the pharaoh could help his people.

Ancient Egyptians believed it was the pharaoh's job to help the sun travel across the sky after his or her death. They thought the sun rose in the morning and set in the evening only with the help of the pharaoh. If the sun did not rise and set, the Nile River would not know when to flood. Without the flood, the rich soil would not help the crops grow and ripen. Everything depended upon the pharaoh and the sun making their **sacred** journey together.

sacred—holy or having to do with religion

CHAPTER 2

PLANNING A PYRAMID

Even a powerful ruler such as Khufu could not build a pyramid by himself. The mind behind the pyramid was most likely Khufu's **vizier**, Hemiunu. Before building could begin, Hemiunu and his engineers had questions to answer. Where would the pyramid be located? When would building begin? How would the pyramid be built?

vizier—an important government official
architect—a person who designs and draws plans for buildings, bridges, and other construction projects

WHO WAS HEMIUNU?

Most of what is known about Hemiunu comes from words carved into his tomb. Hemiunu is thought to be the **architect** of the Great Pyramid. He was Khufu's nephew. He was the top official in Egypt, the one in charge of the practical business of running a kingdom.

A statue of Hemiunu was discovered in his tomb at Giza. The head of the statue was missing, so sculptors created the one shown here.

THE GIZA PLATEAU

Hemiunu built the pyramid on the Giza plateau. Giza is west of the Nile River. Egyptian burial sites were west of the Nile because the sun sets in the west. The Giza **plateau** is made of **bedrock**—a good place for building. It was strong enough to support the massive pyramid. Khufu's father, Sneferu, had built a pyramid on desert sand. The sand shifted, which made the pyramid crack and bend. Hemiunu learned from Sneferu's mistake.

Hemiunu knew there was plenty of **limestone** on the plateau. Workers cut stone for the core of the pyramid there. They did not need to bring as much stone from far away. In fact, a large section of stone jutted out of the bedrock on the Giza plateau. Hemiunu and his engineers used this rock to anchor the pyramid to the plateau. By building around the section of stone, they did not need to cut as much stone for the pyramid's core.

Sneferu's bent pyramid was built on unstable sand.

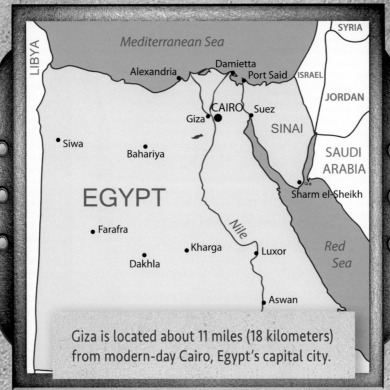

Giza is located about 11 miles (18 kilometers) from modern-day Cairo, Egypt's capital city.

plateau—an area of high, flat land
bedrock—a layer of solid rock beneath the layers of soil and loose gravel broken up by weathering
limestone—a hard rock formed from the remains of ancient sea creatures

THE FLOODING OF THE NILE

The supporting beams inside the pyramid needed to be made of much harder stone than limestone. Granite was brought from a **quarry** in Aswan, 500 miles (805 km) away. Granite is strong enough to support the weight of the heavy surface stones. Hemiunu wanted to cover the outside of the pyramid in beautiful white limestone. This stone was brought from Turah, 10 miles (16 km) away.

Hemiunu sent the stones in boats on the Nile River to get them to Giza. To make sure they arrived safely, he had to know when the Nile's yearly flood began. Moving the stones in boats during the flood would be much easier than pushing or pulling them across land. At the peak of flooding, the river rose to within 1,312 feet (400 meters) of the pyramid site. Lessening the distance of land travel would make the project easier for the builders.

This slab, which depicts Khufu's name, is made of granite.

quarry—a place where stone or other minerals are dug from the ground

Egyptians used the stars to determine when the flood would happen. Sirius, the brightest star at night, appeared in the sky around the same time that the Nile would flood every year. Hemiunu had to have stone cut, ships built, and a harbor ready to meet the rising Nile. If he didn't get the timing right, the project would be delayed by a whole year.

CHAPTER 3

POSITIONING THE PYRAMID

The east side of Khufu's pyramid faces the rising sun. The west side faces the setting sun. The northern and southern sides line up with the Nile, which flows south to north. Most scientists agree that Hemiunu used some form of **celestial** measurement to find the directions.

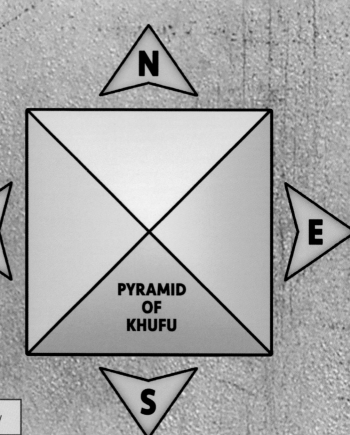

celestial—relating to the stars and the sky

POLARIS STAR

Stars make trails of movement around Polaris.

FINDING THE CELESTIAL NORTH POLE

In today's sky, the star Polaris seems to stand still. The other stars appear to move around it during the night. Polaris marks the direction north. At the time the pyramid was built, 4,000 years ago, two other stars stayed still in the sky. Egyptians may have used those stars to locate north.

LEVELING THE SITE

Once the four directions were marked, the building surface had to be leveled. If one side of the pyramid was higher or lower than the other three, the whole structure might collapse. The Giza plateau is sloped so they did not try to level the bedrock. Instead, they leveled the first layer of stones.

The Egyptians may have used water to level the stones. Flowing water always settles to a level surface. If they cut channels into the first layer of stones, they could pour water into those channels. Once the water settled, they could mark the water line. By cutting along that line, the stones would be the same height. But moving enough water to flood the 13-acre (5-hectare) base would have been difficult.

Recently, **archaeologists** found evenly spaced holes along the east and north sides of the pyramid. Egyptians may have placed posts in these holes. First they would have dug each hole to the same depth. Then each pole was cut to the same height. And cords were stretched between the poles to be sure the stones were the same height.

archaeologists—a scientist who studies how people lived in the past

SQUARE LEVEL

They also used a device called a square level. It has a wooden triangle on top of a long rod. A **plumb line** dangles from the top. The level is set on a flat surface such as a stone. If the stone is perfectly level, the plumb line hangs in the center of the rod. If the plumb line does not hang in the center, the rock is not even and needs to be trimmed. Hemiunu's builders probably re-leveled the layers of stone as the pyramid rose.

This square level currently resides at the Egypt Museum in Cairo, Egypt.

plumb line—a piece of string with a weight fixed to one end; used to test whether something is vertical

MOVING A HUGE STONE

When the design was complete, **stonemasons** began cutting. Egyptians used red paint to mark lines on the quarry stones. Then they used copper tools to cut channels in three sides of the rock wall. They hammered wedges into the channels to break the stone loose from the wall.

Some people wonder how they cut the huge stones when they had no iron tools. Copper saws were too soft to cut through the stone. Archaeologists think the Egyptians poured slurry into the saw cuts. The slurry was made with water, quartz sand, and gypsum. The copper saws and slurry worked together to scrape through the stone. Traces of the slurry were found in stone cracks at Giza.

stonemason—someone who builds or works with stone

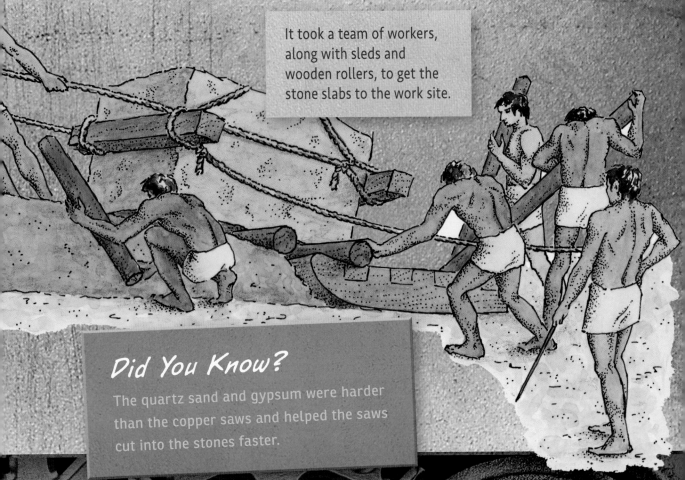

Stonemasons also used a hard pounding rock called dolerite to finish the blocks. Then they used levers to lift them onto wooden rollers. The stones were rolled onto large sleds to be moved to the work site. When the Great Pyramid was complete, it contained 2.3 million stones. They weighed 2 to 50 tons (1.8 to 45 metric tons) each.

It took a team of workers, along with sleds and wooden rollers, to get the stone slabs to the work site.

Did You Know?

The quartz sand and gypsum were harder than the copper saws and helped the saws cut into the stones faster.

RAMPING UP

There are many theories about how the stones were moved into place. Most agree that a ramp was used.

Some say it was a single ramp. But a single ramp would have had to be almost 1 mile (1.6 km) long. If it were shorter, it would be too steep to be able to move the stone. A 1-mile- (1.6 km-) long ramp would need as much building material as the pyramid itself.

Others say it was a zigzag ramp up one side of the pyramid. It is also possible that it was a ramp that spiraled upward. It could have wrapped around the pyramid as it grew. Recently, some scientists have even tried to prove that the ramp was inside the pyramid. The ramp remains an engineering mystery.

This illustration, created in the mid-1900s, shows workers creating a spiral ramp.

PLACING THE STONES

More than 1,000 stones had to be delivered every day to keep the project on schedule. That means, on average, Hemiunu's masons put one stone in place every two minutes.

The largest stones sit at the base, and the stones get smaller and lighter as the pyramid rises. Once the stones were in place, stonemasons trimmed them so they fit very closely. Gaps between the outer stones are so narrow that the blade of a knife cannot fit between them. The stones in the pyramid's core did not fit as tightly as those on the surface. The gaps between the core stones were filled with pebbles.

Did You Know?

The ramps may have had tracks made of talfa, a local clay that becomes slick when wet.

CHAPTER 4

INSIDE THE GREAT PYRAMID

Egyptian pyramids often contained three rooms. In the Great Pyramid, there is an unfinished room deep in the bedrock. Some said this room was supposed to be Khufu's underground tomb. Others point out that the tunnel leading to the room is too small for the **sarcophagus** to have traveled through it. It is possible that the room was used to fool tomb robbers. Or the architects may have changed their design during construction.

a walkway inside the Great Pyramid

Did You Know?

The Great Pyramid is the only ancient pyramid with chambers built above ground level.

sarcophagus—a stone coffin; the ancient Egyptians placed inner coffins into a sarcophagus

THE QUEEN'S CHAMBER

The second room is called the Queen's Chamber. The name is misleading. No queen was ever buried in it. Some people think this room might have housed Khufu's ka statue.

The roof of the room is V-shaped. To work the ceiling beams into place, the builders may have filled the chamber with sand. The sand held up the beams while they were fitted into place. Workers removed the sand when the ceiling was done.

Did You Know?

Khufu's queens had their own, much smaller, pyramids nearby.

ROBOTS EXPLORE THE QUEEN'S CHAMBER SHAFTS

The Queen's Chamber has two shafts that point up toward the surface. These shafts never reach the outside. Scientist Rudolf Gantenbrink used a robotic camera to climb into the shaft and take photos. The photos showed that the Queen's Chamber shafts were plugged! Two blocks, each having two copper pins, were lodged in the passageways. No one knows why. No one knows what lies on the other side of the stone plugs.

THE KING'S CHAMBER

The most important room in the pyramid is the King's Chamber. It would hold the pharaoh's body when he died. It is made of strong red granite, and it contains the red granite sarcophagus. The room is about 34 feet (10.4 m) long, 17 feet (5.2 m) wide, and 19 feet (5.8 m) high. Hemiunu installed nine granite slabs for a roof. They would keep the room from caving in under the weight of the upper pyramid. Each slab weighed between 42 and 50 tons (38 and 45.4 mt). On top of those beams are five more roofs. Each one is separated by an empty chamber to help spread the weight around. The system of chambers and roof beams has kept the King's Chamber safe for more than 4,000 years. The roof of the main chamber is the only one of its kind in ancient architecture.

Did You Know?

The Orion constellation is associated with Osiris, the Egyptian god of the dead.

OPEN TO THE HEAVENS

Two narrow shafts lead out of the pyramid on the north and south walls of the King's Chamber. The northern shaft points directly at the pole stars—stars that line up with Earth's north pole in the night sky. The southern shaft points directly to the constellation of Orion. Without records, we cannot know what the builders intended these shafts to do. They may have been pathways for the King's ba and ka to travel into the sky.

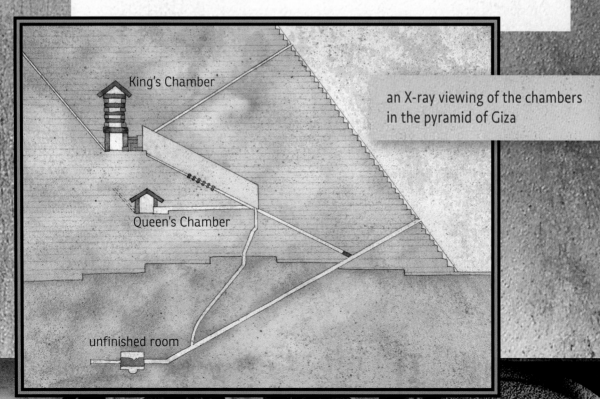

King's Chamber

Queen's Chamber

unfinished room

an X-ray viewing of the chambers in the pyramid of Giza

THE TOP AND BACK DOWN AGAIN

The top piece of the Great Pyramid, or **pyramidion**, was made of solid white Turah limestone. It was the hardest stone to place. There was very little room to move at the top of the pyramid.

Khufu's finished pyramid rose 481 feet (146.6 m) from the sand. It was the tallest structure in the world for 3,871 years. The Lincoln Cathedral in the United Kingdom broke the record in AD 1311.

Once the pyramid was capped, the builders began their descent. They also placed white Turah limestone over the sand-colored stone from the Giza plateau. The white stones fit snugly, giving the pyramid a smooth finish. Workers took apart their **scaffolds** and ramps as they moved toward the base.

The white limestone on the pyramid of Khafre, who was the second son of Khufu, remains intact to this day.

WHO BUILT THE PYRAMID?

Recently, archaeologists discovered a lost city where the pyramid builders lived. Looking closely at human and animal bones, they learned that the workers had been healthy and well fed. When their bones broke, they received good medical care. They even ate expensive beef several times a week.

Stonemasons hid the names of their work "gangs" inside the pyramid. One gang called itself "Friends of Khufu." Archaeologists believe the graffiti shows they were proud of their work.

Heaps of ash and large baking pots were found in the lost city. They also found evidence of beer brewing. This convinced them that the people who lived at Giza were paid for their labor in grain, cloth, oil, beer, and other necessities. The workers were not enslaved, as was once thought.

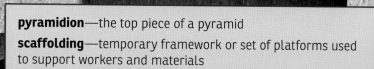

pyramidion—the top piece of a pyramid

scaffolding—temporary framework or set of platforms used to support workers and materials

KHUFU ASCENDS

When Khufu died, his body was placed on a funeral boat. He crossed the Nile, heading west to Giza. His body was mummified and placed in his red granite sarcophagus. The Egyptians believed Khufu would use the Great Pyramid to travel into the sky.

Today, the Great Pyramid of Giza still lives up to its name. Visitors, historians, and engineers marvel at the construction of the Great Pyramid and its long-standing legacy.

Did You Know?

Archaeologists have found ancient texts buried in the pyramids. One of those pyramid texts reads, "The portal of heaven is open for you toward the horizon. The heart of the gods rejoices at your approach."

GLOSSARY

archaeologist (ar-kee-AH-luh-jist)—a scientist who studies how people lived in the past

architect (AR-ki-tekt)—a person who designs buildings, bridges, and other construction projects

bedrock (BED-rahk)—a layer of solid rock beneath the layers of soil and loose gravel broken up by weathering

celestial (suh-LES-chuhl)—relating to the stars and the sky

engineering (en-juh-NEER-ing)—using science to design and build things

level (LE-val)—to make flat

limestone (LIME-stohn)—a hard rock formed from the remains of ancient sea creatures

mummify (MUH-mih-fy)—to preserve a body with special salts and cloth to make it last for a very long time

pharaoh (FAIR-oh)—a king of ancient Egypt

plateau (pla-TOH)—an area of high, flat land

plumb line (PLUHM LINE)—a piece of string with a weight fixed to one end; used to test whether something is vertical

pyramidion (PEER-a-mid-eon)—the top piece of a pyramid

quarry (KWOR-ee)—a place where stones or other minerals are dug from the ground

sacred (SAY-krid)—holy or having to do with religion

scaffolding (SKAFF-old-ing)—temporary framework or set of platforms used to support workers and materials

stonemason (STONE-may-suhn)—someone who builds or works with stone

sarcophagus (sar-KAH-fuh-guhs)—a stone coffin; the ancient Egyptians placed inner coffins into a sarcophagus

vizier (vuh-ZIR)—an important government official

READ MORE

Hoobler, Dorothy, and Thomas Hoobler. *Where Are the Great Pyramids?* Where Is... ? New York: Grosset & Dunlap, 2015.

Jackson, Tom. *Wonders of the World.* DK Eyewitness Books. New York: DK Publishing, 2014.

McDonald, Fiona. *The Egyptians.* Children in History. Mankato, Minn.: Sea-to-Sea Publications, 2011.

INTERNET SITES

FactHound offers a safe, fun way to find Internet sites related to this book. All of the sites on FactHound have been researched by our staff.

Here's all you do:
Visit *www.facthound.com*
Type in this code: 9781491448380

CRITICAL THINKING USING THE COMMON CORE

1. Describe the importance of the Nile River to ancient Egyptians' day-to-day lives and its importance to the construction of the Great Pyramid of Giza. Use details from the text to support your answer. (Key Ideas and Details)

2. The author quotes this passage from the Pyramid Texts: "The portal of heaven is open for you toward the horizon. The heart of the gods rejoices at your approach." What does this passage reveal about how ancient Egyptians felt about death? (Craft and Structure)

3. Suppose archaeologists discovered evidence that the pyramid builders were slaves. Describe the type of evidence you think they would find. (Integration of Knowledge and Ideas)

INDEX